T0077893

PREVIOUS PUBLISHED WORKS

Thoughts Feelings Visions Memories

How to Survive on a Little

I'll Wait

Love Has No Color

Joe's Most Dangerous Mission

(Sequel to I'll Wait)

Who Did It?

The Pirates Who Found Jesus

Thoughts of Mind

A Girl Named

Sarah

(A Miracle for Sarah)

DORIS M. JONES

Order this book online at www.trafford.com
or email orders@trafford.com

Most Trafford titles are also available at major online book retailers.

Print information available on the last page.

ISBN: 978-1-6987-0518-7 (sc)
ISBN: 978-1-6987-0519-4 (e)

Trafford rev. 03/16/2021

Trafford
PUBLISHING   www.trafford.com

North America & international
toll-free: 844-688-6899 (USA & Canada)
fax: 812 355 4082

Contents

Thank You

I want to personally thank everyone who has bought one or more of my books. The written reviews are highly appreciated. The most joy is, knowing how you all enjoy my writing.

The stories are fictional. When I get an idea to write, a title will come into my mind. I usually don't write anything down. One day, I will decide that I am going to write a book with that title. When I start writing, the words just flow.

I won't have any idea of what I am going to write. I just start typing and the words come on the page. For the love stories, I'll Wait and Love Has No Color, when it came to the relationship part, I prayed and asked God to give me the right words and He did. I don't want to write the sexual overtone mess. I want to write to show that love is beautiful the way it is meant to be.

My Poetry book is a compilation of my original poems. I started writing as a young child. I have about ten categories for everyone. There are 132 poems. I thank you for supporting my dream. I gave a tribute to my parents for raising me with love, in my Poetry book.

Introduction

$\mathcal{T}$his story is about a little girl named Sarah who is sent to live with her Grandmother, Mrs. Brown. Her parents have an issue that they need to resolve. They felt it was best for Sarah not to be at home until they decided what to do.

Sarah loves and misses her parents very much. She was with her Grandmother for almost a year. During that time they did not visit her together. And they did not visit her often.

This was very heartbreaking to Sarah and Mrs. Brown, her Grandmother. Sarah was used to doing things with her parents. Her Mom, Beverly used to walk her to school when she would be off work. Sarah missed all of this. All of Sarah's new friends had both of their parents at home and she wanted to be a family again.

She prayed to God that her parents would come to her upcoming birthday party together. Sarah will be turning twelve years old and is very intelligent for her age. All her friends and teachers love her. Sarah does not know that her parents have a great surprise for her birthday. Sarah decided to trust God that her parents would come and take her home.

Chapter 1

Sarah Lives With Mrs. Brown

*S*arah lives with her Grandmother, Mrs. Brown. She is eleven years old and has been living with Mrs. Brown for almost a year. Her parents were separated and stayed in the city. They had only seen Sarah a few times. Both parents were only children and spoiled. They both were used to having their way about things. Sarah missed her parents very much and wished that they would reconcile so she could go home. She loved her Grandmother but she wanted to be a family again.

Mrs. Brown was in her early fifties and in very good health. She was also a very good looking lady for her age. She knew that Sarah missed her parents and had been praying that they would get back together. She loved Sarah so much. Sarah is her only grandchild and she wants the best for her.

Sarah was basically a very happy child. Her twelfth birthday was coming up soon and she had been praying that she would see her parents. She remembers the happy times when they were all together. She wondered why she didn't see them often. This made her very sad. Sarah always thought that they separated because of her.

One day Sarah told Mrs. Brown, "Granny, I really miss my parents and I want to go home. I love you so much but I miss them."

Mrs. Brown hugged Sarah and said, "Honey, I know you miss your parents. They are both brats and don't realize how this is affecting you. I am so sorry that I spoiled my daughter. I love her so much but I should have been a little more firm with her."

"Granny, do you think they separated because

of me?" Sarah asked. "Sometimes I feel like I am to blame."

"Oh no, honey. They love you very much. They were young when they got married and didn't realize that you have to work at a marriage to make it work," replied Mrs. Brown.

"How old were they when they married?" Sarah asked.

"Beverly was twenty and your Dad was twenty-two. They were married two years before you were born. Sometimes people don't stop to think that marriage is a serious thing," Mrs. Brown said.

"When I grow up, I am going to make sure that I am ready to get married," Sarah said.

Mrs. Brown laughed and said, "It's not that simple. When you meet that fine guy and fall in love, you don't want to wait."

"How do you know when you are in love?" Sarah asked.

"Well my dear. You just know. It's a feeling that you get when you meet a guy and you feel attracted to him. You enjoy talking with him and get nervous every time you are around him," Mrs. Brown responded.

Sarah is eleven years old coming up to her twelfth birthday.

"I am going to ask God to send me a good husband so we will be happy," Sarah said.

"Sarah that is the best thing to do. When you pray for things, God gives you good things," Mrs. Brown said.

"Do you think my Mom and Dad will ever make up?" Sarah asked. "It's almost a year now."

"I have been praying for the both of them to realize that it's just not the two of them. They don't realize that their decisions affect you too," Mrs. Brown said.

Sarah said, "Granny, I love you so much and I thank you for taking care of me. You are the best Grandmother in the whole world."

Mrs. Brown said, "The pleasure is all mine. But there are a lot of other Grandmothers in the world, who are considered best."

Sarah said, "I know but you are my best!"

"Thank you for that beautiful compliment," Mrs. Brow said.

They had many fun moments together but it's not the same as having your parents. There will always be a void in a child's life and that is what Sarah is feeling. She knows her Grandmother loves her beyond everything but she misses her parents.

"When I am at school sometimes I get sad because the other children live with their parents. Some of the parents often walk to school with their children," Sarah said. "Mom would always walk with me to school when she was on vacation from her job."

"At least you have some good memories of being with your parents. I believe in prayer and I do believe that they are going to work things out soon. Prayer is powerful and God answers prayers," Mrs. Brown said.

"Granny do you really think so?" Sarah asked. "Do you think it might be soon?"

"Yes, I really think so," Mrs. Brown said. "Did you finish your homework, young lady?"

"I only have a little. I did most of it before I left school. When we have extra time in our last class, I start my homework for the next day," Sarah said.

"You are a very smart young girl. Most children don't think ahead. When I was in school, I used to study a chapter ahead of what we were discussing in class. Sometimes when we got to the next chapter, the teacher would have us to write a report on it. Since I had already studied that chapter, all I had to do was write my report," Mrs. Brown said.

"Now I see where I get my smarts from," Sarah said.

They both laughed and Mrs. Brown hugged her and said, "While you are finishing your homework, I will clean up the kitchen."

"OK Granny. I will do the rest of my homework," Sarah said.

She hugged Sarah and they were laughing as they often do. Mrs. Brown was very concerned about Sarah missing her parents. She didn't want her to go into depression. She often wondered if there was something that she could do.

When Beverly called, she didn't really like to talk to Sarah because she always asked when she could come home. Of course this hurt Mrs. Brown when this happened. Mrs. Brown often told Sarah that she loved her very much and would always be there for her.

Sarah would respond with, "I know you love me and I appreciate you taking care of me but I miss my family."

Now that Sarah's birthday is near, she is wondering if her parents are going to visit with her or send gifts. The gifts don't mean that much to her because she would rather see them. She wants to hug them and hear them say, "I love you,

Sarah." This is a very trying time for her but she doesn't want Mrs. Brown to feel unappreciated. She knows that Mrs. Brown loves her very much.

When Sarah's parent's separated, she was told that she would live with Granny for a little while. Beverly told her that she and Marvin had to work some things out. Sarah had no idea that it would take this long for them to get back together. Beverly had told Sarah to pack a bag because she was taking her to Granny's house.

Whatever the problem was, Sarah knew that her parents could not agree on it. She loved Mrs. Brown and was always happy to be with her but she didn't want her family separated. All the other children had their Moms and Dads at home and she wanted the same. Sarah cried herself to sleep that night. Sarah thought she was the problem.

Mrs. Brown had heard her crying but figured she needed to get it out of her system. Sometime when people have problems, they need a little alone time. Mrs. Brown was very hurt that Beverly and Marvin had decided to separate.

When your children become adults, sometimes you have to hold your peace and let them work things out. Sarah was always a happy child. At school she excelled in her classes and she participated in after school activities. She loved playing softball and tennis. She had many awards for her sports participation as well as her academics.

Beverly stayed in the family home and Marvin rented a room locally. Even though they both were local, they did not visit Sarah regularly. Each one would call Mrs. Brown to see when one of them was planning to visit so they didn't show up on the same day or time. Mrs. Brown had told the both of them that were being foolish and it was unfair to Sarah.

Mrs. Brown did everything that she could to keep Sarah's mind off her problems. She did not want it to affect her grades. Sarah met a lot of new friends which made her happy. She also liked her new teachers but she missed her old friends and teachers. She just wanted to be home again with her parents.

Mrs. Brown and Sarah would go to the movies a couple of times a month. On Saturdays sometimes, they would go to the mall and eat lunch. It was during the night that was hardest for Sarah because her Mom and Dad would spend time with her before she went to sleep. They would take turns reading to her but they both would be there. She knew she was loved and felt very secure.

Sarah loved the relationship that she had with her parents. They always had time to talk with her and answer any questions that she had. When they decided to separate, she was heartbroken.

(As parents, we don't realize what we sometimes put our children through).

Chapter 2

Sarah Misses Her Parents

"Granny, I have decided that I am going to make the best of my situation," Sarah said.

"How are you going to do that?" Mrs. Brown asked.

"Well, I am going to stop focusing on my parents. I am going to study hard and keep getting good grades," Sarah said.

"That sounds like a great plan but what brought this on?" Mrs. Brown asked.

"When you are miserable you don't function well. So I am going to stop being miserable and excel, Sarah said."

"Where did those words come from?" Mrs. Brown asked.

"I don't know exactly but I asked God to help me be a better person regardless of the way things are right now," Sarah said.

"Well you asked the right person. He can help us in any bad situation. I have always known that you were intelligent but I didn't realize how wise you are for your age," Mrs. Brown said.

"I am going to make myself happy. Granny if it's not too much trouble, I would like to learn to bowl," Sarah said.

"That won't be a problem. Actually, I used to bowl a lot of years ago and I was good at it," Mrs. Brown said.

"You did?" Sarah asked.

"Yes and I think that's a good idea. I still have my bowling ball," Mrs. Brown said.

"When can we go?" Sarah asked.

"We can go this weekend and I will teach you," Mrs. Brown said. "It's easy to learn. You will learn in no time."

"Wow! Sarah said, "We are going to have some fun."

They both started laughing. Mrs. Brown knows now that she won't have to worry about Sarah. She thought, "It is going to be fun teaching my granddaughter how to bowl."

All week Sarah was excited and could hardly wait for the weekend. She was going to learn how to bowl and her Grandmother would instruct her.

Sarah mentioned this to her friends, Marsha and Jessica. They were excited for her. They said they were going to ask their Moms to bring them to the Bowling Alley.

Marsha told Sarah, "It would be nice for us to learn to bowl together."

"Yes, that would be awesome," Jessica said. "After we learn to bowl we can join a Bowling League."

Sarah and Marsha said, "That will be fun."

"My Mom knows how to bowl. I will ask her to teach me," Jessica said.

"I am really excited. Maybe we all could go once a week together. Your Mothers can meet my Grandmother and they can take turns taking us to bowl," Sarah said.

"That sounds great!" Jessica and Marsha said.

"Just remember that we have to stay on top of

our studies. We don't want our grades to drop or we may not get to bowl," Sarah said.

"When we have extra time at school,

we can do our homework. That will give us time to study ahead," Marsha said.

"That is a great idea," Sarah said, "My Granny did that when she was in school."

"When I get home, I will talk to Mom about bowling. It will be a lot of fun for us to bowl together," Jessica said

"I will let you all know what time my Granny and I will be going to the Bowling Alley," Sarah said.

"Good," Marsha said, "That way, we can meet up about the same time and our Mothers can meet your Granny."

"Well, my Granny just turned the corner. She is always on time to pick me up," Sarah said. "I've got the best grandmother in the world. See you guys tomorrow. Bye."

Marsha and Jessica waved hello to Mrs. Brown as she drove up. Then they went to sit on the bench to wait for their Moms. Sarah was so excited when she got in the car with Mrs. Brown.

Mrs. Brown asked, "How was your day? You seem extra happy. Did something special happen today?

"I was telling Jessica and Marsha that you are going to teach me to bowl. They were very excited and wanted to learn too. Now they are going to ask their Mothers to bring them to the Bowling Alley," Sarah said.

"That's wonderful," Mrs. Brown said.

"We thought if we all went bowling, then their Mothers and you could switch off taking us each week, if you all don't mind," Sarah said.

"Of course, I won't mind. Then I will get to meet their Mothers," Mrs. Brown said.

"Thanks Granny, you are the greatest and I love you.' (She gave her Granny a big hug). Thank you for always picking me up on time," Sarah said.

Mrs. Brown told Sarah to get Jessica and Marsha's phone numbers so she could call and talk to their mothers about going bowling. Sarah was very excited about this and Mrs. Brown found herself thinking, "We are going to have a lot of fun."

After they got home, Sarah said, "I am going to finish my homework."

"And I will start dinner. It should be ready in about forty-five minutes," said Mrs. Brown.

"Granny, I really miss my parents, My Dad

used to sit at the table with me doing his work, in case I had questions. I really miss that time that I had with him," Sarah said.

"I know honey. They just have some things to work out. Let's pray that it won't be too much longer," Mrs. Brown replied.

"My birthday is coming soon. I would love for them both to come and visit with me," Sarah said.

"Try not to focus too hard on that. You don't want to get side tracked from your school work. You have great grades and you don't want to mess them up," said Mrs. Brown.

"I know Granny. I will stay focused on my schooling and keep my grades up. I will be aiming for several scholarships for college as I get older. Then Mom and Dad won't have to pay a lot of money for my college education," Sarah said.

"That's great! Now to the homework," said Mrs. Brown. "Stay focused on God and He will work it out."

"OK Granny. I am not going to feel sorry for myself.

Homework, here I come," said Sarah. They both laughed.

Mrs. Brown started thinking how she could

get Sarah's parents back together. She decided that she would have a meeting with each of them separately and then both of them together. The main thing was to be able to do this without Sarah finding out. She wanted to try and do this before her birthday.

If what she had in mind worked, both parents would be at Sarah's birthday party that she was planning. The next day Mrs. Brown got busy. First she called Sarah's Mother Beverly. After she set an appointment with her, then she will call her Father Marvin and set an appointment with him.

She has never interfered in their relationship but she feels that she needs too. It's been almost a year since they separated and Sarah has been with her. Sarah is the one who is suffering and she doesn't like it.

Mrs. Brown has been in prayer for Beverly and Marvin. She knows that they still love each but are spoiled and are being simple right now. She has an idea that may help them to realize their foolishness.

She didn't tell Sarah about her plan.

Chapter 3

Marvin and Beverly Met

It was a nice summer day thirteen years ago (in 1999) when Beverly rode her bicycle to the local store. When she was trying to put her lock on it she heard a big whistle. Then she turned around, and saw it was Marvin. She had on bike shorts and it showed her beautiful legs as well as her curves when she stood up.

"What is that for? Don't you have manners?" Beverly asked.

"Yes, I have manners but when I saw you, I could not help myself. You are a very beautiful woman," Marvin answered.

"Is this the first time you have seen a beautiful woman?" Beverly asked.

"Actually it's not but the first time that I saw one that appealed to me," Marvin said. "You are absolutely breathtaking. I mean it. You are truly a natural beauty."

"I am sorry if I responded too abruptly. I didn't mean to be so harsh," Beverly said. "It's that I get so much unwanted attention from the wrong type of men, if you know what I mean."

Beverly could tell that Marvin was different from most of the men who had tried to get her attention.

"In that case I accept your apology and I understand. By the way, I am Marvin. What is your name?"

"It's Beverly. I am sorry but I have to go in the store so I can get back home."

Beverly excused herself and went into the store. She didn't know that Marvin would be waiting for her outside. After Beverly purchased her items and came back out of the store, she saw Marvin near her bicycle.

"Will you have a problem giving me your telephone number?" Marvin asked. "I would like to call you sometime."

Beverly said, "Yes I do and I don't give strangers my phone number."

Beverly unlocked her bicycle and put her bag into her bike basket and went to leave. When she turned her bicycle around Marvin was standing in front of her.

"I live in the neighborhood. May I give you my phone number?" Marvin asked.

Beverly figured if she took it, she would be able to get rid of him. She knew that she would never call him.

"Yes, I'll take it," Beverly said.

"You can call me any time," Marvin said.

Beverly got on her bicycle and went home. When she went to her room, she thought about Marvin and how cute he was but she was smart. She put his phone number in her jewelry box.

A week later, when she was going to her Business Administration class at her college, she saw Marvin going down the hall, two doors from her class. They were attending the local college. She was twenty- one and he was twenty-three years old. Marvin was going to be an

Accountant and this was his last year. Beverly had one more year. He didn't see her as she went into her class.

After Beverly saw Marvin at school, she began to wonder about him. She had never dated because she had not met anyone that interested her. She had girlfriends to do things with and visit. She does things with her parents and goes to church also. Since she met Marvin, she can't stop thinking about him but she won't call him.

Three weeks later Beverly had just driven in the student parking lot and guess who she parked next to? It was Marvin. He had just gotten there and was looking for his parking permit in his glove compartment. When he put it on his mirror, he looked and saw Beverly. Marvin rushed out of his car and went over to her car.

"Good morning, Miss Beverly," he said. "What a surprise to see you here."

"Good morning Marvin. I take classes here too," Beverly said.

"What classes are you taking?" Marvin asked.

"My main class is Business Administration," Beverly answered.

"I am studying to be an Accountant. When I am finished, I plan to open my own business,"

Marvin said. "I have been planning this since I was sixteen years old."

"That's interesting and it is a lucrative business. Will it take a lot of money for you to start your business?" Beverly asked.

"Actually no, since I will be doing the work myself. As I get clients, I will have to hire someone to help," Marvin said, "When I started working as a teenager, my parents let me save all of my money for my business."

"You have been planning since you were sixteen?" Beverly asked. "That's quite impressive. Will you be local?"

"Yes, I am. This is my home and I love it here and my parents are still here," Marvin said.

"That's great! A lot of children move away from their parents when they become adults," Beverly said.

Marvin said, "This is my last year and I am excited."

"Well I have one more year and I am happy. I will wait a year or two before moving out from my parents because I plan to start my own business," Beverly said.

"That's great. What type of business?" Marvin asked.

"Bookkeeping and Business Organization," Beverly said.

Marvin was thinking she is very intelligent. When she finishes school, maybe we can become business partners.

Marvin thought, "I really like her."

"Will you join me for a hamburger after class?" Marvin asked.

"I get out at 2:00 p.m. today. I will go only if you ride with me. You know we are still strangers," Beverly said and laughed.

"I promise to be a perfect gentleman and I will be happy to ride with you. I will meet you by your car," Marvin said.

They parted and went to their classes. Marvin couldn't believe that Beverly had agreed to go for a hamburger with him. He was very excited. In the meantime Beverly could not get him out of her mind.

Beverly thought, "Marvin seems like a very nice person." She was excited too.

This would actually be her first date. When Beverly got out of class and went to her car. Marvin was waiting for her. He was so excited that she was going to eat with him. While he was in class he kept looking at the clock. It seems almost like the time stood still. This was going to be a special day for him because he liked Beverly from the first day that he saw her.

"Have you been waiting for a long time?" Beverly asked.

"Actually I have been waiting only for about two minutes," Marvin answered.

As Beverly unlocked her car, Marvin came on her side to open the door for her. This was a surprise for Beverly. She had always noticed couples when she was out and none of the guys opened the car doors for their women. Beverly realized that Marvin had manners and she liked him.

Just as Beverly was driving out of the parking lot, Marvin asked, "Where would you like to eat?"

Beverly said, "Either MacDonald's or Jack n' the Box."

"Ok, does it matter which one?" Marvin asked.

Beverly said, "No. You invited me so you can decide."

"Since MacDonald's is close, we can go there so we can have more time to get to know each other," Marvin said.

Beverly felt comfortable with Marvin. She thought she would be nervous. They both were at ease with each other. After they got to Macdonald's and parked, Marvin got out and opened the door for Beverly. When they went inside, he pulled her chair from the table for her to sit down. Then he sat down across from her.

"What would you like?" Marvin asked.

"A cheese burger and a Dr. Pepper with no ice will be fine," Beverly said.

Marvin asked, "Do you want fries or dessert with your meal?"

"Thank you but I don't want anything extra," Beverly said.

After Marvin put their orders in, he came and sat down across from Beverly.

"Do you have sisters and brothers?" Marvin asked.

"No sisters or brothers. I am an only child," Beverly answered. "My Mom lost a baby before me."

"I don't have sisters or brothers either. I am an only child also," Marvin said.

"Are you serious?" Beverly asked

"Yes, I am. It's just me," he said.

"What church do you and your family go to?" Beverly asked.

"We go to Grace Community because it's close to the house and it's nice," Marvin answered.

"I just spoke with my parents last week about changing to Grace because it's closer to the house and I like it better," Beverly said. "When we moved her two years ago, my parents wanted to keep going to our church but it's an hour drive one way."

"That can be tiring after a while, especially during the rainy season," Marvin said. "So are you guys coming to Grace?"

"We are planning to be there this coming Sunday," Beverly said. "Did you grow up in this area?"

"Yes and I love it here because it's a family neighborhood and everyone is friendly," Marvin said. "By the way are you seeing anyone?"

"No, I am not seeing anyone. What about you? Are you seeing anyone special?" Beverly asked.

"I am not seeing anyone either. I am a loner and I don't really date," Marvin said.

"Why don't you date?" Beverly asked

"Well, I just never met anyone that I thought might be compatible to me. But now I think we may be compatible," Marvin said,

"So you feel like we are compatible?" Beverly asked.

"Actually you are the first lady that I approached voluntary. When I saw you, I just felt that you were special," Marvin said. "It was a feeling I had, so I spoke to you."

"For your information, I normally don't take strangers phone numbers," Beverly said, "and I was never going to call you."

"Why did you take it?" Marvin asked.

"So you wouldn't keep trying to get my phone number and you would leave me alone," Beverly said.

"Look at the time. I have to get home. I have a test tomorrow and I need to go over my notes. It's been nice being here with you," Marvin said.

"I have enjoyed talking with you. You are different and I think you are nice. Thanks for inviting me," Beverly said.

"You are more than welcome. Maybe we can go to a movie sometime," he said.

"We will see," she said. Her thoughts were, "Guard your heart. You have to take your time and not rush things. He is very nice and likable."

As Beverly drove Marvin back to school so he could get his car, she thought that he might be a nice person to socialize with. She pulled into the school parking lot and parked next to his car.

"Thank you again, Marvin for inviting me. I will see you tomorrow," Beverly said.

"The pleasure was mine. Be careful driving home. See you tomorrow," Marvin said.

As they parted, they realized that they had a very good connection with each other. They had a lot in common and enjoyed their conversations. There are about to be some interesting events and changes in their lives. Neither one of them have ever been in love before. These new feelings they are having are about to take over in their lives. When Beverly got home her Mom was in the family room. Beverly went in and sat beside her on the couch.

Beverly said, "Hi Mom."

"Hi Sweet heart. You are a little late today. Is everything alright?" Mrs. Brown asked.

"Yes everything is fine. I was invited for a hamburger at MacDonald's by a school friend," Beverly said, "His name is Marvin Garner."

"Oh!" Mrs. Brown said as she turned to Beverly smiling.

"Marvin is cute and very polite. He said he

doesn't date because he had never met anyone that interested him," Beverly said.

"Marvin sounds interesting. What are his plans when he finishes school?" Mrs. Brown asked.

"Well, this is his last year and he plans to open his own Accounting Business. He has everything set up," Beverly said.

"That sounds like a responsible man and one who knows what he wants," Mrs. Brown said.

Beverly said, "Yes Mom. He is very interesting. He grew up in this area. Marvin and his parents go to Grace Community Church."

"I am glad that you have met a nice young man. Just be careful and pay attention to everything. Most of all guard your heart," Mrs. Brown said.

"Thanks Mom. I will be careful. I am going and lay down before I study," Beverly said. "I want to make sure to keep my grades up and stay on the Honor Roll."

"Beverly, your Dad and I are very proud of you and appreciate the person that you have become. We love you dearly," Mrs. Brown said.

"You guys are the greatest parents and I love you both with all my heart," Beverly said. "I have always tried to carry myself in a nice way so you all would be proud of me. I thank both of you for being good parents," Beverly said.

"Well with you, it was easy. No parent could ask for a better child," Mrs. Brown said.

"I could not have had better parents. You and Dad are the best," Beverly said. "Mom, I will talk with you later. Love you."

"Get you some rest. Love you," Mrs. Brown said.

Chapter 4

The Courtship

$\mathcal{S}$ince Beverly and Marvin met, she had someone to do things with. She liked the simple things in life, going to the park, the beach, basketball games, etc. She was not looking for a relationship because she had never been in love nor had a strong crush on anyone. Beverly was very naive in a lot of ways but happy with her life.

Beverly told her parents about Marvin and asked if it was alright to invite him to dinner one evening. Mr. and Mrs. Brown were excited because they were beginning to think that Beverly might not ever marry.

Mrs. Brown asked, "How old is he and does he live close by?"

Mom, he is twenty-two years old and he lives ten minutes away. Marvin is also an only child," Beverly said.

"Does he go to church?" Mr. Brown asked.

"Yes Dad, he goes to Church and he has good manners too," Beverly responded.

"How soon do you want to bring him home?" Mrs. Brown asked.

Beverly said, "I will wait a little while but I will give you plenty of notice."

"That sounds like a plan but we want to meet him before you start going out with him," Mr. Brown said.

"OK Dad," Beverly said.

Every day now, Marvin and Beverly talked to each other in between their classes. After about two weeks, Marvin wanted to see more of her.

He has gotten used to seeing her every day at school now and in two days it will be Friday. This is going to be a three day weekend for President's day. When Beverly got out of class, he was outside of her classroom.

"Hi. How was class today?" Marvin asked.

"It was good. I always try to learn something new each day," Beverly said.

"What are you going to be doing over the week-end?" Marvin asked.

"I will probably just kick it around the house. I don't have any plans," Beverly said.

"I don't have any plans either. I was wondering if you would like to go to the movies this week-end?" Marvin asked.

"Well, that would be nice but you will have to meet my parents first," Beverly said and then laughed.

"Is your Dad a real tough man?" Marvin asked and laughed.

"He's a sweetheart. He won't scare you. My parents just like to know my friends," Beverly said.

"Ok, now we have that out of the way, which day is better, Friday or Saturday?" Marvin asked.

"Saturday will be good for me. I guess I should give you my phone number and address," Beverly said.

"And what time to pick you up?" Marvin asked.

"I am still living at home so I will have to be

home by midnight. Is 6:00 p.m. too early for you?" Beverly asked. "You can come to dinner and we can leave about 7:00 or 7:30 p.m."

"That's great. Is it alright if I call you tonight?" Marvin asked.

"It's ok. You can call me any time after 6:00 p.m.," Beverly said.

They were walking to her car. When they got there, Marvin went to her side of the car so he could open the door for her. He was glad that he met Beverly. Now he would have someone to hang out with. After they said good-bye, while driving home, Beverly was thinking about how nice Marvin was. She was glad that she accepted the date with him.

When Beverly got home, she told her parents that she accepted a movie date with Marvin for Saturday so she invited him to dinner first.

Her parents looked at each and both said, "That was quick." They all laughed.

Saturday seemed like it took forever to come. Marvin was getting a little nervous. He had dated a couple of girls before but neither one of their parents had asked to meet him. He realized that Beverly's parents were concerned about who she was going to be dating.

On Saturday Marvin arrived at Beverly's house at exactly 6:00 p.m. When he rang their door bell, she was shocked that he was so punctual. He didn't want to be late and he wanted to make sure they had time for her parents to check him out. Mr. Brown went and opened the door. Marvin's parents had taught him the importance of being punctual.

"Hello young man. You must be Marvin!" Mr. Brown said.

"Yes Sir, I am. How are you today?" Marvin asked.

"Fine, thank you. Come on in. Beverly will be in shortly," Mr. Brown said. "Take a seat."

"Thank you, Sir," Marvin said. "Your home is beautiful."

"Thank you, Marvin," Mr. Brown said.

Mrs. Brown entered the room and Marvin stood up. She was surprised at his manners.

"Honey, I want you to meet Marvin," Mr. Brown said. "By the way, what is your last name?"

Marvin said, "It's Garner, Sir."

"I am pleased to meet you, Marvin," Mrs. Brown said.

"Thank you ma'am, the pleasure is mine," Marvin said.

"Marvin, you seem like a well raised young man. When you take my daughter out, I expect for you to have her home no later than midnight," Mr. Brown said.

"That's not a problem Sir. I will honor your Request," Marvin said.

"Also, I expect for you to respect my daughter and protect her from all hurt, harm or danger if possible," Mr. Brown said.

"Mr. Brown, you don't have anything to worry about. Your daughter is a beautiful person and my father has showed me how to treat a woman. He loves my Mother and treats her like she is the only person in the world," Marvin said.

Just as he finished that sentence, Beverly came into the room. She was more beautiful than ever.

"Hi Marvin, I see you have met my parents," Beverly said.

"Yes and they are as nice as you," Marvin said.

"I prepared dinner but since you all are going to the movies, you can come back a little early and eat. Sometimes it's hard to get a good parking and a good seat in the theater," Mrs. Brown said.

"Dad if you don't mind, we will leave now and come back a little early," Beverly said.

"You all have a good time and be careful. Marvin, are you a licensed driver with car insurance?" Mr. Brown asked.

"Yes Sir and I obey the law," Marvin said.

Beverly kissed her Mom and Dad good-bye.

"It was nice meeting both of you and thank you for allowing me to take your daughter out," Marvin said.

"You are welcome," replied Mr. Brown.

Mr. Brown closed the door as Beverly and Marvin left. He turned to Mrs. Brown.

"Our baby has grown up. She is a young lady now," Mr. Brown said.

"I know. Where did the years go?" Mrs. Brown asked.

"Marvin seems well mannered and nice," Mr. Brown said.

"Yes he does seem like a nice young man," Mrs. Brown said. "After Beverly sees him a few times and thinks she likes him, we can invite his parents over for dinner."

"That sounds like a good idea," Mr. Brown said.

In the meantime, Marvin and Beverly went on their way to the movies.

"Would you like to get something to eat before

going in the movies or eat at your house after the movie?" Marvin asked.

"I would rather eat afterwards if you don't mind but we can get a couple of small snacks. Maybe candy bars or peanuts," Beverly said, "Or small bag of chips."

"That sounds great to me," Marvin said, "Then I can eat some of that good food your Mom cooked."

They stopped at the store and got one small bag of chips and two candy bars and put them in Beverly's purse. Her purse wasn't that big so the Attendant would never suspect that she was bringing any food items in the movie.

When they got to the movies, there was a small line, but they did not have long to wait before going in. The movie that they were going to see was a mystery type movie. They enjoyed being together. They found out that they have a lot in common.

After the movie, they stopped at a MacDonald's close to Beverly's home. It's only five minutes to her home. After they bought sodas, they sat down and talked to learn more about each other. The movie had ended a little early, at 9:30 p.m. They had not planned to go to her house until about 10:30 p.m. While at MacDonald's they enjoyed their talk. They found out more things about each other and the more they found out, the more they liked each other. It wasn't crowded, so they did not have to rush to leave.

"What do you do in your spare time?" Beverly asked.

"I am a home body. I usually read or listen to soft music. Sometimes I hang out with a couple of buddies of mine," Marvin said.

"What kind of music do you like?" Beverly asked.

"I like mostly all music but jazz is my favorite," Marvin said. "So what do you like doing?"

"I am basically a loner but I have two girlfriends to do things with sometime. I am at home a lot because I like being at home," Beverly said.

"When you were growing up, did you ever wish for sisters or brothers?" Marvin asked.

"Oh yes. There were times when I didn't like being the only child but I adjusted," Beverly said. "At one time I used to dream about having a sister."

"I know the feeling. But I had a good life. Do you think we can do this again?" Marvin asked.

"I don't see why not. I have enjoyed being

with you and thank you for a pleasant evening," Beverly said.

"It was most enjoyable for me too. In the summer we can go to the beach or boardwalk," Marvin said.

Beverly said, "I would love too. I like walking on the beach and feeling the sand on my feet but I don't like for them to get wet though."

"You are like me on that. I don't like muddy feet. I think it's time for me to take you home," Marvin said, "I don't want your Mom to feel like I didn't want to eat her cooking. Actually, I am looking forwards to it."

"Again, I thank you for a nice evening," Beverly said.

"You are very welcome and I thank you for a lovely evening too," Marvin said.

When he pulled up in front of her home, he parked the car. He got out and went around and opened her door, then took her hand to help her get out of the car.

When they went inside, Beverly looked at the clock. It was only 10:20 p.m. Her parents were still up watching a movie on T.V.

"I will heat the food for you all," Mrs. Brown said as she got up off the couch.

"Did you all enjoy your movie?" Mr. Brown asked.

"Yes Sir, we did. It wasn't over- crowded and we got good seating and parking. I thank you and Mrs. Brown for trusting me to take Beverly out," Marvin said.

"Son, you are very welcome," Mrs. Brown replied, as she fixed their plates.

Mr. and Mrs. Brown kind of listened as Marvin and Beverly sat, ate and talked. They realized that they had a lot in common and seemed to really enjoy each other.

"Beverly may have found a rare jewel. He is a very nice young man," Mr. Brown told Mrs. Brown.

"I agree with you. He is genuine, thank God," Mrs. Brown said.

After Marvin and Beverly finished eating, he helped Beverly clean up. This impressed all of them. Marvin left their house about 11:45 p.m., after he thank the Browns again. As he was driving home, he kept thanking God for meeting Beverly. He thought her parents were nice too.

Beverly thought, "I really enjoyed Marvin's company. He wasn't boring and he has good manners. I am glad Mom and Dad like him."

On Marvin's ten minute drive home he was thinking, "I have never liked a girl like this before. Maybe we will have a real relationship. I really enjoyed her this evening and her parents."

As time went on, Marvin and Beverly were spending more time together. Almost every week-end, they would go to different places. They liked the same things so it was never a problem of where they would go or what they would eat. They were at the park one Saturday and Marvin noticed most of the guys were with a girlfriend. This was about four months after they met.

Marvin said, "Beverly, I love spending time with you. I will be graduating in a couple months and I will be very busy for a while setting up my business."

"I have been thinking about you leaving school soon. I am going to miss you. I have never had a friend like you before," Beverly said.

"Will you be my lady?" Marvin asked. "I know that we have only known each other for about four months and I don't want to lose you."

Beverly said, "Yes I will be your lady but I have a stipulation. As long as we are not married, no sex."

He said, "I believe I can honor that."

Before he realized it, he was hugging and kissing her. She wrapped her arms around his neck and returned his kiss. They kissed for a long time. When they stopped kissing, both of them started laughing. They realized that they had fallen in love.

That following Sunday, Beverly and her parents went to Grace Community Church. Finally they got to meet Marvin's parents. When Marvin saw Beverly and her parents, he lit up like a light bulb.

"Mom, Dad this is Mr. and Mrs. Brown, Beverly's parents and this is Beverly," Marvin said.

Mr. Garner said, "I am Jim and this is my wife Nancy. We have heard so much about all of you."

Mrs. Garner said, "We are very delighted to meet all of you. Please call me Nancy."

We have been looking forwards to meeting you all," Mrs. Brown said, "And call me Deborah. This is my husband David."

"You have raised a fine young man," Mr. Brown said.

"Thank you. We did our best to teach him the right way," Mrs. Garner said.

"You can truly be proud of him," Mrs. Brown said.

Marvin's parents both said, "Thank you," at the same time.

"We are happy to finally meet you all. Marvin talks so much about Beverly. He has never had much interest in any one girl before," Mrs. Garner said.

"It looks like the feelings are mutual. Beverly had never dated before. She had not been interested in anyone until she met Marvin," Mrs. Brown said.

"We are just happy that her interest is in a worthy young man, if you know what I mean," Mr. Brown said.

"We know. Parents always worry if they are going to like that special someone your child brings home," Mr. Garner said. They laughed.

"After we met Marvin, we knew that we could breathe," Mr. Brown said. "We must get together some evening for dinner or something."

Chapter 5

Business Partnership Proposal

$\mathcal{M}$arvin and Beverly started spending all of their free time together. Mr. and Mrs. Brown were very happy that Beverly had met a nice man. They liked Marvin because he was polite, intelligent, well dressed and good looking.

Mr. Brown told Mrs. Brown, if Marvin and Beverly got married, they would have good looking and smart grandchildren.

As it was coming up to Marvin's graduation, he began to think about Beverly being his business partner, (50-50). He decided to propose this to Beverly. They had plans just to hang out today so he felt this would be a good time to discuss it. They would not be rushed and she didn't have to give him an answer today.

After Marvin picked Beverly up, he drove to the park. They didn't have any particular plans. They just wanted to be together. After they found a nice spot, he opened his IPAD.

"Beverly, I've gotten an idea and I want to run it by you to see what you think," Marvin said.

"OK," Beverly said.

"What do you think of us going into business together as fifty-fifty partners?" Marvin asked. "I don't want you to answer right now. Talk it over with your parents and see what they think about it."

Beverly asked, "Are you serious? Wow!"

"Yes I am very serious. We get along well and I trust you and think we can have a great and successful business together," Marvin said.

"That sounds very interesting but how much money would I need?" Beverly asked.

Marvin said, "You don't need any money

right now. We can have a contract that after you graduate, as you make money, you can make payments on half of what it cost me to open the business. I am going to open the business next month. We will have to choose a name for the business quick."

"Marvin, I am honored that you want me as your business partner. We can be great together. How soon do we need to come up with a name?" Beverly asked.

"I plan to file it in two weeks and open the door two weeks after that. In the meantime, you can work part-time in the office until you graduate," Marvin said. "This way you will already know everything about the office. Also, I would like for you to help me set up the office."

"I would love to do that. I will discuss it with my parents. In the meantime, put a contract together. I am sure my Dad will want to read it," Beverly said.

Marvin said, "As our business grows, we can hire some college students to work part-time. We will be able to do Income Tax, Business Taxes for other businesses, Typing, etc. I can see great potential in this business. You can also incorporate Business Organization in it. We can actually register both businesses."

"So you are planning to have our business opened by the time you finish school. That is so surreal," Beverly said." Now I will need a name for my business."

"Since I have spent money to open, I want to start making money right away. I have about six committed clients waiting," Marvin said. "If you have a name for your business, we can register them at the same time. We will have a Corporation name and it will cover both businesses. The way the office is designed, is perfect. You will have your office on one side and mine will be on the other side."

"Marvin, you are a very smart man," Beverly said.

"Yes I am and you are a very smart woman. That's why I want you as my partner. We can make a lot of money," Marvin said. "If your parents want to talk with me before you sign the contract, let me know."

"This is so exciting. Thank you for wanting me as your business partner. You won't be sorry," Beverly said.

"Would you like to see your Business Office?" Marvin asked.

"You mean you have the space already?" Beverly asked.

"Yes and I have the keys," Marvin said. "Let's go!"

Beverly was so excited. She was thinking that, "He is the right man for her. This is truly a blessing and I will make him proud of me."

When they got to the office, it was in a very good location. Beverly was so happy and it was a beautiful building. Marvin gave her a set of the keys to the office. She could not believe it. Beverly was very excited about their office.

"You are giving me keys before I sign the contract?"

Beverly asked.

"Well, I am usually a good judge of people. I would trust you with my life," Marvin said.

Beverly hugged and kissed him. She just could not believe it. She doesn't know it but he is planning to propose to her when she signs the contract. Marvin wants to wait until she graduate before marrying her. He wants Beverly to stay focused and finish her schooling.

When Beverly got back home, she was full of joy and excitement. Mrs. Brown came into the family room where Beverly was and sat down.

"Are you alright?" Mrs. Brown asked.

"Mom, I am so happy. Where is Dad?" Beverly asked.

"David is in the garage. He will be in shortly," Mrs. Brown said.

"Tell me about your day and what has made you so happy. Did Marvin propose to you?" Mrs. Brown asked.

"No Mom but I will wait until Dad come in so I can tell both of you, my good news!" Beverly said.

Just as Beverly finished her sentence, Mr. Brown walked in and asked, "What good news do you have? Did Marvin propose to you?"

Mrs. Brown and Beverly started laughing.

"No Dad. Sit down and I will tell you what happened," Beverly said. "Marvin asked me to be his partner, fifty-fifty. He is planning to open his door in a month. Marvin will give me a contract but he wants you all to read it before I sign it. Today he took me by our office. After we got there, he gave me a set of keys," Beverly said. "My own set of keys to the office.

Beverly proudly held up her keys with a big smile on her face.

"How much money is he asking you for?" Mr. Brown asked.

"Marvin has paid for everything. He said I can work part-time in the office until I graduate. After I am working full time, I can make payments on half of what it cost to open the office," Beverly said.

"Is he for real?" Did he say how much it cost to open the office?" Mrs. Brown asked.

"No but he told me not to stress over it and it won't take a life-time to pay my part," Beverly said. "I will be earning half of the profits. We are going to incorporated both of our businesses under a Corporation."

Mr. Brown said, "I am anxious to see this contract and the agreement in it. That's a brilliant idea to Incorporate. That way it will cut both of your costs. This man is smart beyond his years."

"Mom, Dad, he told me his plans on all the different ways we will be able to make money in the businesses," Beverly said. "Marvin said he would be happy to meet with you all if you felt it necessary."

"I could tell that he is very intelligent just from talking with him. He sounds like a genius," Mr. Brown said.

"Marvin has been saving and planning for this since he started working at sixteen. He said he had enough saved where he did not have to borrow money," Beverly said.

"Wow! That's a smart person," Mrs. Brown said. "Pray about it. We will read your contract and let you know what we think but the decision will be yours. Whatever you decide, we will stand by you."

"Thank you, Mom and Dad. You guys are the best. I will take my time and read the contract. Marvin said, it will not be complicated and it will be easy to understand," Beverly said.

Mr. Brown said, "I can tell that you really like him. Just be careful and don't rush things."

"Dad, Marvin is the nicest man that I know beside you. I am in prayer about our relationship. He understood when I told him that I am not willing to have sex unless I am married," Beverly said.

"What did he say to that?" Mr. Brown asked.

"He told me that he can live with it," Beverly said.

Mrs. Brown said, "Looks like our daughter has found a good man who knows how to respect and treat a woman".

Chapter 6

The Wedding

*M*arvin and Beverly continued to spend all of their spare time together. Now it's apparent that they are in love. Since Marvin graduated he has been working on their business. Beverly will be graduating in a couple of months. They are excited about being partners in their businesses. They decided to name their businesses, "Financial Services and Office Organization."

Mr. and Mrs. Brown thought this sounded like a wedding might be in the works. Sure enough,

Marvin was already making plans to ask for Beverly's had in marriage. He wanted to talk with her parents before proposing to her. He made a date to see them when Beverly was at school. Marvin told them that he needed to discuss something with them.

When Marvin got to Beverly's home, he became nervous as he rang the doorbell. Mr. Brown opened the door and said, "Come on in son."

Marvin said, "Thank you, Sir. How are you today?"

Mr. Brown replied with, "I am great. How are you?"

"Fine, thank you," Marvin said.

Mrs. Brown was already sitting down in the family room. When Marvin came in the room, she stood up to greet him.

"Hi Marvin! Would you like something to drink? Water or juice?" Mrs. Brown asked.

Marvin said, "Water will be fine, thank you."

After Mrs. Brown brought Marvin the water, they all sat down."

Marvin said, "I came to ask permission to marry Beverly. I am very much in love with her and I want to marry her. I didn't want to ask her until I got your approval. I am planning a special date for this weekend to propose."

Mr. Brown jumped up and said, "Son, we love you and know that Beverly loves you. You have our blessings. We have prayed about this and believe that you all will be very happy together."

After Mr. Brown hugged Marvin, Mrs. Brown hugged him and said, "We will be proud for you to be part of our family."

"I thank both of you," Marvin said. "I have told my parents my plans. Mrs. Brown, I would like you to help with our wedding plans."

"It will be my pleasure son," Mrs. Brown said.

Marvin was shaking and tears were rolling down his face. Mrs. Brown hugged him again and her eyes watered.

"I guess I had better go. I will be picking Beverly up after class. I thank both of you very much. Please, not a word to Beverly," Marvin said.

"Nooo! We won't spoil your surprise for her. Be safe," Mrs. Brown said.

Mr. Brown walked him to the door. As Marvin left, he looked back and waved at Mr. Brown. He was so happy that they approved of him. Beverly had become his everything. He loved her so much.

When Marvin got to the school to pick Beverly up, he was still nervous and excited. She was going to be his wife. When Beverly came out of the school, he couldn't wait to hug her. As she neared the car, he rushed to her and just held her.

"Is everything alright? You are shaking. Marvin has something happened to one of my parents or yours?" Beverly asked.

"Everything is fine. That's what you do to me. I love you so much. You have been on my mind all day. I am happy to see you," Marvin said.

"Wow! Marvin, I love you too. When I am apart from you, I am lost," Beverly said.

Marvin kissed Beverly just as she finished speaking. This was the only place where they kissed in public, the school parking lot. After kissing Beverly, he just held her.

"I think we should go before we get an audience," Beverly said.

They started laughing. He opened the car door for her to get in. He then went to the driver's side, got in and closed the door. Marvin sat starring at Beverly.

"Honey, you can't imagine how much I love you. You are that one gem in the middle of a batch of raw diamonds," Marvin said.

"Thank you for that compliment but I hope you know that you are special too, at least to me," Beverly said while laughing.

"I have a special place that I would like to take you Saturday night," Marvin said.

"Well, since I spend all of my free time with you, I think I just might be available," Beverly said. "Just tell me what time to be ready and I will be waiting."

They started laughing. Marvin started the car and took Beverly home. Just as Marvin pulled up in front of Beverly's house and turned the motor off, he turned and looked at her.

"You just don't know how happy you have made my life," Marvin said.

His eyes watered. Beverly gently touched his face.

"Marvin, I have never been in love before and the way I feel about you, I know it is love. When we are apart, I can hardly wait to see you again," Beverly said.

"If we weren't in front of your parent's home, I would kiss you again but I think you had better get out. Call me later," Marvin said.

He got out of the car and went to the other side to let Beverly out. Such a gentleman, she thought.

"Alright and keep those tears out of your eyes. I love you very much. Talk to you later," Beverly said.

It was only two days before Marvin was going to ask Beverly to marry him. They both had busy schedules but the time passed fast. Marvin called Beverly on Saturday and told her what time he would pick her up.

Beverly was so excited because she had never been in love and Marvin was just perfect for her. It was like she was counting the minutes when they would be together again. They both were very comfortable with each other. When Marvin arrived, Beverly was ready. Just as he was about to ring the doorbell, she opened the door.

"Good timing," Marvin said.

"You are very punctual. That's a very good virtue and I love it," Beverly said.

They laughed and Beverly took Marvin's hand and they went to his car. Marvin opened the passenger door for Beverly and went to the driver's side and got in.

Marvin said, "Well, as he looked at Beverly, how was your day?"

"It was great but it's better now that you are here," Beverly said.

"I missed you too. I am taking you to a very special place. I hope you like it," Marvin said.

"Since you chose it, I am sure I will love it," Beverly said.

They did small talk until they arrived at the place. Beverly had never been here before. It was a small restaurant in a nice part of town. After Marvin parked the car, he got out and went to the passenger side to let Beverly out.

"This is nice. I haven't been here before," Beverly said.

"A friend of mine told me about it. I thought we might go somewhere different. Well, let's go in and check it out," Marvin said.

As they enter the front door, the Hostess took them to a private section of the restaurant. It had a candle lit on the table and it was a round cubicle. There was a bouquet of roses on the table also. Marvin seated Beverly and then he sat across from her. In the background they could hear their favorite song.

When Beverly heard the song, she looked at Marvin and said, "What a coincident. They are playing our favorite song."

"How about that! This is nice," Marvin said.

(She didn't know that he had already arranged everything.)

The waitress brought them menus and asked if they wanted something to drink before ordering.

Marvin said, "Please bring us some water."

Beverly was looking at the menu.

"Do you see anything that you might like?" Marvin asked.

"I would like the meatloaf, mashed potatoes and green beans. It's been a while since I had meatloaf," Beverly said.

"That sounds good. I think I will have the same," Marvin said.

When the waitress brought their water, Marvin gave her their orders.

Marvin said, "This is nice and cozy. I like it."

"It's romantic and special. I like it to," Beverly said.

After they received their food and finished eating, the waitress came and cleared their table. The waitress asked if they wanted any dessert.

They both said, "No thank you," at the same time. They were full from the dinner. Then Marvin turned to Beverly after he took a little box out of his pocket.

"Beverly, you have become the light in my life and I have fallen deeply in love with you," Marvin said.

Beverly's hand covered her open mouth. She was not expecting this and her eyes watered.

"Will you marry me?" Marvin asked.

"Oh, my God! Are you sure?" Beverly asked.

"I am very sure. Will you marry me?" Marvin asked.

Beverly said, "Yes! Yes!

The waitress and people in the booths near them started laughing and clapping. They both got up at the same time and hugged each other and kissed.

"I love you so much. I want to spend the rest of my life with you," Marvin said.

"I will be happy to be your wife because I am in love with you," Beverly said.

Before they left the restaurant, they thanked everyone.

As Marvin was driving her home, he said, I have already talked with your parents and got their permission to marry you."

"When did you do that?" Beverly asked.

"Two days ago. They were very excited and I asked them to not say anything to you," Marvin said.

"Well, they didn't slip anything. I was so surprised. Wow! They knew you were planning this and they did not act suspicious at all," Beverly said.

"When can we set the wedding date?" Marvin asked. "I am hoping that we can get married the weekend you graduate."

"That sounds good to me. I don't like being away from you," Beverly said.

After they got back to Beverly's home, they went inside.

Mr. Brown asked, "How did it go?" And smiled.

Marvin said, "She said, "Yes."

Mr. and Mrs. Brown hugged and kissed both of them.

"When is the big date?" Mrs. Brown asked.

"We will have a double celebration. It will be the weekend that I graduate from school," Beverly said.

"We don't want anything extravagant. We want a nice small wedding with family and a few friends. "Since we just opened the businesses, we want to be economical," Marvin said.

"That makes money since to me," Mr. Brown said. (They laughed).

"I have to leave now and I thank both of you for your beautiful daughter," Marvin said.

"You are very welcome and we are glad it's you." Mr. and Mrs. Brown said at the same time. They all laughed.

It was only about two and a half months until Beverly's graduation. She and Mrs. Brown had gotten busy making the plans with Mrs. Garner. It's now late spring 2000. They have a short list of guests to invite and the reception will be at the Browns house. They have a beautiful backyard.

Mrs. Brown and Mrs. Garner picked out a beautiful white wedding dress for Beverly. It wasn't a wedding gown but an eloquent dress. Beverly fell in love with it. The food would be finger food and they would decorate the backyard with ribbons and balloons.

As it got closer to Beverly's wedding day, she got more nervous. She realized that she had never been with a man and was wondering about that after the wedding. She wasn't sure of how things were to happen and didn't want to be embarrassed. One day she pulled her Mother, Mrs. Brown aside to ask a question. This was a very personal question and she wasn't sure how to ask it.

"Are you alright, honey? Is there a problem?" Mrs. Brown asked.

"Yes but I am very nervous," Beverly said.

"What are you nervous about?" Mrs. Brown asked.

"You know, the wedding night," Beverly said.

Mrs. Brown laughed and said, "Honey don't worry about that. You will know what to do."

"Mom, it's not funny. I have never been with a man before," Beverly said.

"Honey, God gave us natural instincts. Believe me, you will be alright," Mrs. Brown said. "Don't worry! The man is just as nervous as the woman. You all will get to know each together. Now let's finish up with this decoration."

Well June 22, 2000 finally came and Beverly was a nervous wreck. She had gotten her hair done. Beverly's hair was very long. She had curls on both sides perfectly pinned to her head, a big ball in the middle of her head. She was a beautiful bride. When Marvin saw her, he almost fainted. He was so happy.

Mr. Brown was so proud of his daughter. She was intelligent, beautiful and loving. Mrs. Brown already had tears in her eyes. Mr. Brown assured her, "That Beverly had met a very find young man. We don't have to worry about her because he is in love with her."

"I know we are getting a great son-in-law. I am just so happy," Mrs. Brown replied.

As Beverly was walking to be joined with her future husband, she felt like crying. She was so in love with Marvin. He could not take his eyes off of her as she came to him. He was so nervous and began to shake a little. They both were smiling with tears in their eyes.

Before the Pastor starting going through the vows, Marvin held up his hand.

"Beverly, I want you to know that I have never been in love before. I love you more than life itself and one promise I want to make and that is, no matter what happens, I will always love you," Marvin said.

Beverly was so moved by what he said that her knees almost gave way under her.

"Marvin, I love you with all my heart and I can match your vow because I have never been in love before and no matter what happens, I will always love you," Beverly said.

By now everyone was wiping their eyes including the men. It was such a great romantic moment. Finally the Pastor did the vows. When Marvin raised Beverly's veil, he said, "I love you, Mrs. Garner."

Then he kissed her like he had never kissed her before. It was so long, everyone started laughing and clapping.

After the kiss, the Pastor said, "I want to introduce Mr. and Mrs. Marvin Garner."

The crowd went wild with congratulations and laughter. Everyone started hugging and kissing them. They had a short reception and finally slipped out and went to the hotel. They decided not to go on a honeymoon because Beverly had just graduated and the businesses were newly opened a year ago and business was picking up fast. She also wanted to hire two part-time helpers and one full-time helper because she wanted to make sure they would be able to have time together. Mrs. Brown used to work as a Receptionist and she said if they needed her, she would be glad to help out.

Mrs. Brown was hired as permanent full time Office Manager. She would oversee the other workers and help wherever she was needed. Besides, she loved working again because it kept her busy. Sometimes she would be able to pick Sarah up from school.

Chapter 7

Mr. Brown's Heart Attack

When Sarah was almost eleven years old, Mrs. Brown had called Beverly to tell her that her Dad was ill. She said she had rushed him to the hospital and was in the emergency room. As soon as Beverly got off the phone she told Marvin that her Dad was in the emergency room.

"What's wrong with him?" Marvin asked as he was putting on his shoes.

"I don't know. Mom just said she had to rush him to the hospital and they are in the emergency room." Beverly said.

Beverly asked her neighbor to watch Sarah until they get back. When she and Marvin arrived at the hospital, Marvin let Beverly out at the door and he went and parked the car. When Mrs. Brown saw Beverly, she broke down in tears.

"Your Dad has had a heart attack. The doctors don't know how serious it is," Mrs. Brown said.

Beverly started crying. Then Marvin came in and saw the two women hugging each other and crying together. Marvin looked at both of them and got weak in his knees. He thought Mr. Brown had passed.

"Mom, what happened to Dad?" Marvin asked.

Mrs. Brown stopped crying and hugged Marvin.

"Honey, he had a heart attack and they don't know the severity of it," Mrs. Brown said.

"I am so sorry Mom. Come and sit down and try to relax. We don't want anything happening to you," Marvin said.

They all sat down and began to pray together. After they prayed, Marvin told Mrs. Brown that Mr. Brown was in good hands.

"I know that God is in control and we have to trust Him no matter how bad things seem," Mrs. Brown said.

"Mom, we are here and we will stay all night if necessary. Sarah is next door with my neighbor. Marcy told me not to worry about Sarah. She said if we needed to stay all night, it is alright," Beverly said.

"I hate to see my husband in pain," Mrs. Brown said. "I have never seen him like that before."

"Mom, we have to keep praying for the best and ask God to help us deal with whatever is to be," Beverly said.

"We have been married for twenty eight years and I still love my husband. I don't want to lose him. He is a very good man," Mrs. Brown said.

"I know Mom. He's been a good father also. We both love him very much. It would really break Sarah's heart to lose her grandfather," Beverly said.

"Now, both of you stop talking like that. We don't know the outcome. Just keep praying if it's God's will for him to recover," Marvin said.

Just then the Doctor came into the waiting room. They all jumped to their feet. Mrs. Brown was the first one to speak.

"Doctor is my husband going to be alright?" Mrs. Brown asked.

"Right now, it's hard to tell. It's bad but we are doing everything that we can to try and save him," the Doctor said.

"Thank you, Doctor for your honesty," Marvin said.

"It's going to be a long night. You all may want to go to the Cafeteria and get some coffee to calm your nerves. I will let you all know if there is a change," the Doctor said.

"Thank you, Doctor," Mrs. Brown said.

Marvin and Beverly went to the Cafeteria and got coffee for all three of them. Mrs. Brown would not leave. She wanted to be there if there was a change in her husband's condition.

As the time passed, Beverly and Marvin kept calm as Marvin was trying to assure Mrs. Brown that Mr. Brown would probably pull through. It was about 3:00 a.m. when the Doctor came through the door. When they saw the Doctor's face, they knew it was bad news.

Marvin got up first. Mrs. Brown was holding her hand over her mouth. Beverly stood up and grabbed Marvin's arm. The Doctor looked at Mrs. Brown as she turned to him.

"I am so sorry. We did everything we could to save him. His attack was severe," the Doctor said.

Mrs. Brown fainted and Marvin caught her before she fell to the floor. Beverly was hysterical, pacing back and forth. Marvin was crying as he attended to Mrs. Brown.

"I will send the Nurse to give Mrs. Brown a shot to calm her," the Doctor said."

"Thank you, Doctor, it will help," Marvin said.

Beverly finally came over to Marvin and hugged her Mother. He had gotten Mrs. Brown in a chair.

Mrs. Brown opened her eyes and said, "Thank you, Lord for giving me a good husband and letting me have him this long."

Marvin prayed for her and asked God to give her and Beverly the strength to endure the pain.

"How are we going to tell Sarah?" Beverly asked.

"It will hurt her but she will be alright. We all will be alright," Marvin said.

The Nurse came and asked Mrs. Brown, "Do you want to stay overnight in the hospital? I can put you in a room and give you a sedative."

"Thank you but I don't need the sedative and

I will go home. If I take a sedative, I will still have the pain when it wears off. I am fine, thank you kindly. I would like to see my husband now, please," Mrs. Brown said.

The Nurse took all three of them to see Mr. Brown's body. They cried and prayed and cried. Mrs. Brown told them that she would come back later to make arrangements for Mr. Brown's body to be moved. They left the hospital about 4:45 a.m. and went home. Mrs. Brown stayed the morning with Beverly and Marvin.

Later that morning Beverly picked Sarah up from Marcy's about 10:00 a.m. When Sarah saw Mrs. Brown, she went and gave her a big hug.

"Where is Papa? Why didn't he come with you, Granny?" Sarah asked.

Everyone looked at each other and Mrs. Brown and Beverly started crying.

"Come here, baby. Your Papa was ill. Granny took him to the hospital. His heart was bad and now he is gone to heaven," Marvin said.

Sarah started crying and hugging her dad. He held her close and told her to remember what they have taught her about death. When she stopped crying, she went to her Granny and hugged her real tight. Then she went to her Mom and hugged her. This was a very sad day for Sarah and her family.

"Daddy, I remember what you told me about death. I know Papa is with Jesus. I love him so much and I am going to miss him," Sarah said.

"Baby, we all are hurting right now but it will get better. We will never forget Papa," Marvin said.

"We all are going to miss him very much. We are going to take Granny home so she can change and make arrangements for Papa's burial. I spoke with Marcy and she will keep you until we get back," Beverly said.

"O.K. Mommy," Sarah replied. "I will be alright." She wiped her eyes.

Marvin picked Sarah up and gave her a kiss on the cheek and hugged her.

"That's my girl. I love you so much," Marvin said.

"And I love you, Mommy, Granny and Papa so much. I am going to miss Papa for the rest of my life," Sarah said.

"Honey, we all are going to miss him forever. He was such a great father and husband," Beverly said.

"And grandfather," Sarah said.

"And grandfather!" Marvin said and they all laughed. "Remember the good times with Papa."

"Now we have to get you next door so we can take Mom to get some things," Beverly said.

After they took Sarah next door to their neighbor, they got in the car to take Mrs. Brown to her home.

"This is going to be real hard getting used to my husband being gone. I never thought that one day we would not be together. I figured we would love each other until death and we would go together," Mrs. Brown said.

"Mom, I cannot imagine the pain that you are going through. My heart hurts for you. I know we all will be hurting but each person has their own special pain," Beverly said.

"I never saw it that way but it is so true. Each person suffers differently in situations like this," Marvin said.

"This is one thing in life that you can never be prepared for. We know one day we all must go but there is no preparation for this journey. You just love, enjoy and respect each other while you can and be happy," Mrs. Brown said.

"Here we are," Marvin said.

Marvin got out of the car and opened the

doors for Mrs. Brown and Beverly. Then they walked toward the front door. Just as they reached the door, Mrs. Brown stopped.

"Mom, are you alright?" Beverly asked. Now she is worried about her Mother.

"I am fine, honey. It just hit me that my husband will never walk through this door again," Mrs. Brown said. "Well, let's go inside."

After they got inside Beverly and Mrs. Brown broke down crying at the same time. It hit both of them like a lightning bolt that they would never see Mr. Brown again.

When Beverly stopped crying, she said, "I had the greatest father in the world. He was my hero."

Marvin was trying to hold back his tears. He walked into the kitchen as the tears flowed down his face. He wanted to be strong for his wife and Mother-in-law but he was hurting too. He and Mr. Brown had gotten very close and he loved him like a father.

"I want to stay with you all for a couple of weeks after the funeral. I know that I am going to dread coming back to this house by myself. I just need a little time to adjust and make this transition," Mrs. Brown told Beverly.

"Mom, you are more than welcome to stay

with us as long as you want and need too. We love you and will support you in any way we can. Besides, Sarah will be excited to have you with us for a while. Marvin can check on your house for you. Just let your neighbor, Mrs. O'Brien know you will be with us for a while," Beverly said. "Give her our number."

"I will call her tomorrow and let her know what's happened," Mrs. Brown said. "Let's get out of here. I don't want to keep crying."

Just then, Marvin walked into the room.

"I have been going through the house to make sure all the windows and doors are locked. I will drop by each evening after work and get your mail," Marvin said.

"Marvin, I really appreciate and thank you very much, Mrs. Brown said. "I am ready to leave now."

"OK, let's go," Marvin said.

They got in the car and went back to Beverly and Marvin's home. No one was trying to make conversation on the way back. Things will be different with Papa gone. Sarah will really miss him.

Chapter 8

The Marriage Split

arvin and Beverly have built their businesses and have a lot of repeat customers. They have been working very hard to establish themselves. Since Mrs. Brown lost her husband, she had been working in their business to help out and to keep busy. She became their permanent Part-Time Office Manager and Receptionist when needed.

Mrs. Brown normally worked four hours a day. They had a room set up where Sarah could lay down after Mrs. Brown picked her up from school. She was working four hours but was paid for eight hours.

The Customers liked Mrs. Brown because she treated them with personal interest. She would ask how they were and their family and greeted them with her beautiful smile. Marvin and Beverly were very happy about that. As time went on Mrs. Brown noticed a difference in their relationship with each other.

One day Mrs. Brown asked Beverly, "Are things alright with you and Marvin?"

"No Mom, they are not." Beverly answered as she looked at her Mom,

Mrs. Brown said, "I am not trying to pry but I have noticed a difference with you guys."

"It's OK Mom. I probably should have said something because I knew that you would notice it after a while. I am beginning to wonder if we got married too soon," Beverly said.

"Well as long as you have been married, I think it's a little late for that thought," Mrs. Brown said. "What seems to be the problem?"

"Actually, I am not sure. I don't know if we are putting too many hours into the businesses or not. He wants to expand but I don't agree right now because of Sarah. I don't want to be away from her no more than I already am," Beverly said.

"I can understand that but you all need to take time and sit down and go over all of the "pros and cons" of the businesses," Mrs. Brown said.

"I think Sarah has noticed that things are different but she has not talked about it," Beverly said.

"Children are very smart and they notice everything, even if they don't speak about it," said Mrs. Brown.

"Actually we have talked about separating for a while," Beverly said.

"You have to be kidding," Mrs. Brown said. "I hope you all will pray about the situation and consider what it will do to Sarah."

"Mom, I just think we need some time apart. We still love each other but right now, it's not working out," Beverly said. "In fact, we were wondering if Sarah could stay with you for a little while."

"That's not a problem but I hope you all know what you are doing. Start preparing Sarah this week so she will have time to prepare herself to live with me," Mrs. Brown said.

"Thanks Mom. We appreciate you," Beverly said.

"How much time do you all think you will need to straighten this mess out?" Mrs. Brown asked.

"Maybe 4-6 months. Hopefully we can get to the bottom of the problem and solve it," Beverly said.

"That means she will have to change her school. This could be a bad experience for Sarah," Mrs. Brown said. "Break it as gently as you can to Sarah."

"We are praying that it won't be. We love her and she knows that we would never do anything to purposely hurt her," Beverly said. "We have agreed that we will not get involved with anyone else to complicate matters. Besides we know that we still love each other very much."

"Well, that's good news. I am glad you all realize what not to do so it won't complicate things for you. That's a very smart decision," Mrs. Brown said. "It's sad that most people don't think like that when they have problems and separate."

"We feel if we keep the focus on us and our problem, we will be able to work it out. Neither one of us want a divorce. We agree no matter what, that won't happen," Beverly said.

"It will be nice having Sarah with me as I make this adjustment in my life. You all know Sarah will be in good hands," Mrs. Brown said. "I will be praying that you guys can work this out. I really don't like you all separating."

"Mom there is no need to worry. I am not going to lose my husband over a disagreement. If I have to give in, I will because I truly love him. If we can't work it out, I will give in," Beverly said.

"That's smart thinking. I love you all so much. Just put it in God's hands and let Him work it out for you," Mrs. Brown said.

"I will be staying at home and Marvin will rent a room. Sometimes we will carpool so the office staff won't be aware that there is a problem," Beverly said.

"That's a good idea. The less people know about your personal business, the better," Mrs. Brown said.

Chapter 9

Bowling Night

$\mathcal{M}$rs. Brown decided to call Jessica and Marsha's mothers to introduce her-self to them. She called Jessica's Mom first.

"May I speak with Mrs. Mitchell?" Mrs. Brown asked.

"This is she," answered Laura Mitchell

"This is Sarah's Grandmother, Deborah Brown," said Mrs. Brown.

"How are you? I have heard so much about you from Jessica," said Laura Mitchell.

"I am planning to start teaching Sarah how to

bowl. The girls have a plan and I am calling to see if you are willing to participate," Mrs. Brown said.

"Call me Laura. Actually, Jessica and I were just talking about it. I think it's a great idea," Laura Mitchell said.

"I am happy that you like their plan. You can call me Deborah or Deb," Mrs. Brown said.

"Marsha's Mother and I are friends. Her name is Norma and we will be happy to join you and Sarah.

The girls can learn bowling together," Laura Mitchell said.

"This will be great. I will call Marsha's Mom and introduce myself. We can start this week-end if you don't have any other plans," Mrs. Brown said.

"We don't have any plans and that will be fine," Laura Mitchell said.

"Well it's been nice talking with you. I will now call Marsha's Mom and see if she will be free this week-end. I will talk with you later and I look forwards to meeting you," Mrs. Brown said.

"It's been my pleasure. Have a good night and thank you for calling," Laura Mitchell said as she hung up the phone.

"You have a good night too," Mrs. Brown said.

After Mrs. Brown finishing talking with Laura Mitchell, she called Norma Davis, Marsha's Mom. The phone rang twice and Marsha picked up.

"Hello Marsha. This is Mrs. Brown. Is your Mom available?" Mrs. Brown asked.

"Just a moment, please," Marsha said.

Marsha put Mrs. Brown on hold and went and got her Mom. Marsha was very excited.

"Mom! I think it is Mrs. Brown, Sarah's Grandmother," Marsha said.

Norma Davis went to the phone. She said, "Hello."

"This is Deborah Brown, Sarah's Grandmother. How are you?" Mrs. Brown asked.

"Fine thank you," Norma Davis said. "Marsha told me that you might be calling."

"Well, it seems that Sarah, Jessica and Marsha have been talking about learning to bowl. They have gotten a plan together so I am calling to see if you are game," Mrs. Brown said.

They both laughed and Norma Davis said," I am game. Marsha has told me about their plan. Since the girls are good friends, it will be nice for us to be friends as well."

"I spoke with Jessica's Mom Laura and she is in. So we can set a date to get this ball rolling,"

Mrs. Brown said. "We need to decide if we want Friday or Saturday night. Either one is good for me and Sarah."

"Either one is good for me and Marsha," Norma Davis said.

"OK, we can start this Friday if you don't have any plans," Mrs. Brown said. "Laura said it was good for her and Jessica. We will see you all Friday. Now I am excited. Bye for now."

Norma, Marsha's Mom called Laura, Jessica's Mom. Laura answered the phone.

"Hey girl, I just got off the phone with Deborah, Sarah's Grandmother. We want to start bowling this Friday. She said you all will be available," Norma Davis said.

"We sure will. We are already cleaning off my bowling gear. This is going to fun teaching the girls to bowl," Laura Mitchell said.

"Deborah said she is excited too. I think we have found us a great new friend," Norma Davis said.

The next day at school the girls were so happy and giggly all day. They are all in the same classes. Now they can't wait for Friday. They are planning to start studying together so they can do their work ahead, in English and History.

Sarah told Marsha and Jessica, "If more children would study ahead, they would be better students. It's a challenge to see how well you do and it can be fun."

"I never looked at it like that but you are right. It can be fun," Jessica said.

"It's like testing yourself to see how many "A's" you can get. I like this idea," Marsha said.

These girls are on a mission, not only to learn how to bowl but learn how to be better students.

"As we go higher in school, we can earn scholarships to college and our parents won't have to pay a lot of money," Sarah said.

"Wow! Sarah, you are smart," Jessica and Marsha said at the same time. They all laughed.

"We all are smart. We are just learning to use our brains better," Sarah said.

They all lived in the same neighborhood and only about two blocks from the Bowling Alley. This meant that they can walk to the Bowling Alley unless it's raining. The adults were just as excited as the girls. They could hardly wait for Friday.

The grown-ups had talked about buying the girls their own bowling balls, shoes and bags once they learned to bowl. This is going to be a surprise for them. The women will go shopping together to buy the bowling gear for the girls. When they arrived at the Bowling Alley, they met up in the lobby. After hugging and greeting each other, they went and secured a lane. They had arrived a little early so they could get a good lane.

Once they secured their lane, they put their balls on the conveyer and put on their bowling shoes. They were ready to go. Mrs. Brown asked if they mind her praying before they started bowling. Everyone reached for a hand. They all held hands as Mrs. Brown prayed. It was a short prayer thanking God for allowing them to meet and to be able to teach the girls bowling.

The girls did the hand thing to see which one would be first. Marsha won so she and her Mom went to the lane. In the meantime, Mrs. Brown had Sarah aside explaining how to pay attention to the arrows on the lane and that there is body posture as you get ready to throw the ball.

Laura had Jessica on the other side of the table explaining bowling techniques to her. Norma demonstrated to Marsha how she was to hold the bowl, then take a few steps to the edge of the lane and roll the ball. She explained that you don't throw it like some people do. When they started,

Mrs. Brown and Laura told Sarah and Jessica to watch how Laura was teaching Marsha.

When Marsha rolled the first ball it went into the gutter. Laura told her to relax and lightly roll the ball down the lane using the arrows as a guide.

"You are aiming to strike. You can't hit the pin straight on. Roll the ball where it will hit the main pin and the one next to it," Laura Mitchell said.

As the night went, the girls took turns bowling and loving every minute of it. They all hit the gutter on the first try but they slowly got the hang of it. They have learned to smoothly roll the ball rather than throwing it down the lane. The ladies were laughing at how they were posing their bodies. The girls did good after they learned their stance better. When Mrs. Brown got up to direct Sarah, she bowled first and got a strike.

"Wow! Granny you can bowl," Sarah said.

"It's been years since I bowled in a league. I am going to enjoy bowling again," Mrs. Brown said.

"After we get the girls bowling, we can get a lane next to them so we can bowl too," Norma said.

"That's a good idea," Laura and Mrs. Brown said.

They spoke at the same time. They all started laughing. They all were having a nice time.

"I am glad the girls thought of this. It's good to get out of the house every once in a while," Norma Davis said.

"I didn't realize what I was missing," Mrs. Brown said. "I am going to get my ball and shoes out."

"This is perfect for me and Jessica to do together," Laura Mitchell said.

"I am glad that we met. I know we will enjoy each other's company," Mrs. Brown said.

"The pleasure is ours. We always hear the girls talking about Sarah's Grandmother. We thought you were much older. You are still young and look good for your age," Laura Mitchell said.

"That's true and you don't look like a Grandmother," Norma Davis said.

"I thank both of you for the compliments," Mrs. Brown said.

"You are welcome," Laura Mitchell and Norma Davis said at the same time and they laughed.

"The girls are smart and kids learn fast. I bet they will be bowling within a month," Norma Davis said.

"I am very happy that Marsha, Jessica and Sarah are friends. They are very nice young girls," Mrs. Brown said.

"Sarah is a sweetheart herself. I fell in love with her the first time I met her, " Laura Mitchell said.

"Yes and she is very polite and naturally nice," said Norma Davis. "We love her too."

"I am glad we all got to meet. I am going to be looking forwards to this every week," Mrs. Brown said.

"I think I am more excited than the girls," Laura Mitchell said.

"They are doing pretty good now. Not many gutter balls," Norma Davis said.

"I knew that they would catch on fast because they are competitive," Laura Mitchell said.

"Sarah told me that they would be doing their homework in advance so bowling won't interfere with their studies," Mrs. Brown said.

"Jessica and Marsha respects her a lot because she is a leader and comes up with good creative ideas," Norma Davis said. "Jessica is always talking about her."

"I told Marsha that Sarah is the right kind of person to have as a friend. It's important to be with people who want the good things in life," Laura Mitchell said.

"Well, I listen to Sarah talking about both of them. They all are very wise for their ages and I believe that they will be very successful in life," Mrs. Brown said.

"But will they find husbands on their level?" Norma Davis asked. They all laughed.

They had been at the Bowling Alley for three hours.

"OK young ladies it's time for us to start packing up. You don't want to over-do it on the first night," Mrs. Brown said.

"Here is something you guys can be thinking on and that is to see if each one of you can get one strike next time," Norma Davis said.

"That's a great idea. You all did very well for the first time," Laura Mitchell said.

All three of the girls hugged each of the ladies and thanked them for bringing them to bowl. They are excited about bowling and probably will be bowling very good by the end of the month. After they turned in their balls and shoes, they headed for home. The girls giggled and chatted on the way talking about how much fun they had.

Marsha and Jessica lived on the same street as Sarah but one block past her home. There is a cross street to divide their blocks. Jessica lives two houses down from Marsha on the opposite side of the street. They got to Sarah's home first and they all said good-night. After the others went past the cross street, they said good-night.

The following Monday at school, Sarah, Marsha and Jessica couldn't wait to see each other. They were still wired up from bowling Friday night. That was great excitement for the girls. Now a couple of their other school friends wanted to know why they were so excited.

Lisa Collins said, "What did you all do that was so exciting?"

"We went bowling and now we are learning to bowl. It was so much fun," Jessica said. "When we get better, we are going to join a league."

"Did you all go bowling down from your homes?" Sherrie asked.

"Yes, we did!" Sarah responded. "Why do you ask?"

"I always wondered what it would be like to learn to bowl. Every time we pass by there, I look over there," Sherrie said.

"I heard it is a nice place," Lorraine said. "I think I would like to learn to bowl."

"My Mom told me when I am older she will teach me how to bowl," Lisa said.

"We all are about the same age. If you guys can learn, we can too," Sherrie said.

"I am going to ask my Mom if she will take me bowling Friday," Lisa said.

"Will you guys be going every week?" Lorraine asked.

"Yes. After we learn to bowl, we are going to get on a league," Marsha said.

"Wow! That sounds like fun," Sherrie said. "I am going to ask my Mom to take me too."

"That will be extra great. We can learn together but you all will have to do what we do," Sarah said.

"What is that?" Lisa asked.

We study ahead so we don't get behind in our lessons," Jessica said.

"Since we all live close to each other, maybe we can form a study group for two hours on Saturdays," Sarah said.

"That's a grand idea. Maybe we can take turns studying at each other's homes," Lisa said.

"We need to get Sarah's Grandmother and our parents together and see if they will agree with us," Marsha said.

"Now we won't be bored anymore," Jessica said. They all laughed.

"I think we need to pray about this. Is this ok with all of you?" Sarah asked.

They all said, "Yes."

Sarah prayed and asked God to bless all of them. She prayed that they would continue to be good friends. And that all the parents would agree to their plan. When she finished praying they hugged each other. Now it was time for them to go back to class. Sarah started thinking about her parents. She thought if she was with her parents, that her Mom would be involved in this. She had to clear her head because she did not want any distractions from her studies."

After school was out, Sarah could hardly wait to tell her Grandmother what she and the girls had discussed. As Mrs. Brown came around the corner, Sarah said good-bye to Jessica and Marsha. When Mrs. Brown stopped to get Sarah, Jessica and Marsha waved at her. Mrs. Brown hugged Sarah as usual when she picked her up from school.

"So what kind of day did you have?" Mrs. Brown asked Sarah.

"I had a wonderful day. You won't believe what happened today," Sarah said.

"Tell me what happened," Mrs. Brown said.

"Well we have three more friends who want to learn to bowl," Sarah said.

"The more the merrier," Mrs. Brown said.

"Lisa Collins, Lorraine Temple and Sherrie Watson are going to talk to their parents tonight. We were thinking maybe we could form a study group on Saturdays. And we could switch off meeting at each other's homes, if their parents agreed to it," Sarah said.

"Are any of your friends behind in their studies?" Mrs. Brown asked.

"No Granny but we figured if we start bowling, that we would do that so we don't get behind in our studies," Sarah said.

"That's smart thinking. Whose idea was that?" Mrs. Brown asked.

"Well I suggested it because studying together we could drill each other and stay on top of things," Sarah said. "That way we all would get good grades."

"That's how you get ahead. I am so proud of you," Mrs. Brown said.

"Thanks Granny," Sarah said.

"What do you want for dinner? I didn't cook today. I thought we might get some fast food," Mrs. Brown said.

"Subway sandwiches sound good to me. I would like a meatball sandwich," Sarah said.

Mrs. Brown said, "Subway it is. I think I will have a tuna sandwich. Since we are already out, we might as well go and get them now."

"We both can get a twelve inch sandwich and eat half now. When we get hungry later, we can eat the other half," Sarah said.

"That sounds like a winner. I think we will pick up some chips too. We still have some Sun Tea for drinks," Mrs. Brown said.

"Sounds good to me," Sarah said.

After they got their sandwiches and chips, they headed for home. Mrs. Brown and Sarah often played checkers and cards to pass time in the evenings. Sometimes they read the Bible together or watch movies before Sarah's bedtime. Sarah really enjoyed her Grandmother but she missed her parents so much.

The next day at school when Mrs. Brown dropped Sarah off, all five of her friends were waiting for her.

"What's going on? Is everything alright?" Sarah asked.

"Everything is fine," Marsha said.

They said, "We are waiting for you." They laughed.

"We are just excited about bowling. We are anxious to start," Sherrie said.

"We talked with our parents last night and they think it's a great idea too," Lisa said. "They want to speak with your Grandmother to make sure it's ok."

"That's no problem. My Grandmother said, "The more the merrier," Sarah said. "I will give you all our phone number. Your parents can call or just come to the Bowling Alley on Friday about 6:00 p.m.

Sherrie, Lisa and Lorraine's Mothers called and spoke with Mrs. Brown before the next Friday. They agreed to meet in the lobby of the Bowling Alley. When Friday came they all were at the Bowling Alley and the girls were overjoyed seeing each other.

"We need to get two lanes so it won't take too long for each of the girls to bowl," Mrs. Brown said. "After another week, we can start switching them off with each other."

"After they start bowling better, they can compete against each other in teams," Joyce Temple said.

"This is going to be exciting to see," Mary Watson said.

"When Sarah mentioned to me about bowling, I think I got as excited as she was," Mrs. Brown said. "I used to bowl years ago. I don't know why I didn't think of it."

"I did too," Norma Davis said. "After we get the girls broke in, we can get us a lane and bowl too."

"Alright you are talking my language," Denise Collins said.

"We are talking good times now," Mrs. Brown said. "Thank God for good company."

They all said, "Amen!"

Chapter 10

Marvin and Beverly Made Up

*M*rs. Brown loves Sarah so much and she enjoys their conversations. Lately, she has been praying about her parents getting back together. Sarah will be twelve years old soon. It's been almost a year since her parents separated. She feels it's been long enough for them to know what they want to do.

Mrs. Brown decided that she was going to give

them a little help. She was going to call and make appointments to meet with Marvin and Beverly on different days. She originally had planned to meet with Marvin first but decided to meet with Beverly first.

She called their office. The receptionist answered on the first ring and said, "Financial Services and Office Organization. May I help you?"

"This is Mrs. Brown, Mrs. Garner's Mother."

"How are you, Mrs. Brown?" The Receptionist asked.

"I am fine. Thank you for asking. Is Mrs. Garner available?" Mrs. Brown asked.

"One moment and I will connect you. Have a good day," the Receptionist replied.

"Thank you and you too," Mrs. Brown said.

When Beverly picked up the phone, she said, "Hello Mom. Are you and Sarah alright?" She asked.

"Yes. We both are fine. I am just checking in with you about our lunch date next week," Mrs. Brown said.

"That is still good. Will 12:30 p.m. be good for you, Mom?" Beverly asked.

"Yes it is." Mrs. Brown answered.

"Do you want to come here or go to a restaurant?" Beverly said.

"I prefer a restaurant so we can have some alone time," Mrs. Brown replied.

"OK, text me and let me know which restaurant and I will be there," Beverly said. "I love you Mom and tell Sarah that I love her too."

Mrs. Brown said, "I love you too and I will relay your message to Sarah."

After they got off the phone Beverly thought it would be nice to have lunch with her Mother. They had not had much time together since her Father passed. She will let Marvin know that she will be out of the office for a couple of hours on Tuesday. They always make sure that one of them was always in the office. Mrs. Brown called Marvin on his cell phone. She didn't want Beverly to know that she was going to make a lunch date with him also.

Marvin answered his phone and Mrs. Brown said, "Hello son. How are you doing?"

"Mom what a pleasant surprise. Is everything alright with you and Sarah?" Marin asked.

"Everything is fine. I was just calling to see if you could have lunch with me on Friday. I want to talk with you about something. Please don't tell Beverly," Mrs. Brown said.

"Are you sure Sarah is alright?" Marvin asked again.

"Sarah is fine. I just want to update you on her. She is doing exceptionally well in school. Besides, I haven't seen you in a little while. I miss you," Mrs. Brown said.

"I am so sorry that I haven't visited you and Sarah more often. I will be happy to have lunch with you. I love you too Mom," Marvin replied.

"Is Johnny's Restaurant four blocks from your office at 12:30 p.m. Friday alright?" Mrs. Brown asked.

"That will be perfect. I have a call and I will see you then. Bye Mom," Marvin said.

"Bye son," Mrs. Brown said.

Of course Mrs. Brown never told Sarah about her plan. She wanted to see if maybe, she could talk some sense into Sarah's parents. She didn't know how these lunch dates were going to work out. She had been praying that they will be able to agree on things and reconcile.

Mrs. Brown was feeling good when she picked Sarah up from school. She was very hopeful that she would be able to get her parents to see how their separation is hurting Sarah. Marvin and Beverly don't have the slightest idea that Mrs. Brown had a plan. She is going to give them some adult wisdom and pray that they will take it in stride.

Sarah is getting more excited about her birthday coming up. She wants both of her parents to come to her party that Mrs. Brown has planned for her 12th birthday. Finally Tuesday came and Mrs. Brown met her daughter Beverly for lunch. They drove up in the parking lot almost at the same time. Beverly thought, "I am punctual just like my Mother." They were able to park next to each other. Mrs. Brown was excited to see her daughter. When Beverly got out of her car, she ran to her Mother.

"Mom it is so good to see you. How is Sarah?" Beverly asked.

"Sarah is great but she misses her parents very much," Mrs. Brown replied.

"I know she does because we miss her. I have been praying that Marvin and I can work out situation soon," Beverly said.

"That's what I want to talk to you about," Mrs. Brown said.

They held hands as they went inside the

restaurant. The booth they sat in was small and away from everyone else. They ordered a light lunch.

After they finished eating, Mrs. Brown said, "Beverly, you are my only child and I miss you."

"I know Mom, I miss you too. We have been very busy at work lately. I will make an effort to see you and Sarah more often," Beverly said.

"What plans do you and Marvin have for Sarah? It's going on a year since you all separated."

"Mom, Marvin and I have been talking. We are getting back together and we are going to do it before Sarah's birthday," Beverly said.

Mrs. Brown shouted, "Halleluyah! I have been praying for you all to reconcile. Thank you, Jesus."

"When Marvin and I separated, we agreed that we would not get involved with anyone else to complicate matters. We both have honored that agreement," Beverly said.

"I am so proud of both of you and I love y'all very much," Mrs. Brown said.

"We want to plan a surprise party for Sarah's twelfth birthday," Beverly said. "And we will apologize to her for what we have put her through.

This will be her real birthday gift. We are calling it A Miracle for Sarah," Beverly said.

Mrs. Brown started crying. She could not hold back the tears, she was so happy to hear this news. Beverly's eyes watered.

"Mom, don't cry. I am sorry we put you and Sarah through this," Beverly said. "Marvin and I love each other very much. We just got a little off track."

"This is one of the happiest days of my life since your Father passed. He would be so pleased. Now I have to hold my tongue with Sarah so I don't spoil her surprise," Mrs. Brown said. I was going to give her a party but I will let you all take care of that. It will be extra special to Sarah," Mrs. Brown said.

"It's time for me to get back to the office. It has been a pleasure to have lunch with my Mom. We will have to do this more often like we used too. I love you so much," Beverly said.

"It was pleasurable for me too. You know that I always love spending time with my favorite girl," Mrs. Brown said.

As they headed for the parking lot, both of them were thinking that this day was a day to remember. On her way home, Mrs. Brown was so excited but kept thinking, how she was going to keep this from Sarah for another two weeks. She knows when Sarah finds out this will be one of the happiest days of her life.

As time went on, Sarah didn't talk so much about her parents. She focused on her school work, sports, and bowling. She had gotten real good bowling, in a short time. Jessica and Marsha learned quickly also. Mrs. Brown had gotten a list of Sarah's friends so she could get the list to Beverly. As time got closer to her birthday, Sarah started wondering if her parents were going to show up. If so, would they be together? She had no idea of the surprise that was in store for her.

Mrs. Brown took Sarah shopping so she could buy her a dress for her birthday party. Sarah was very excited and wasn't sure what type of dress she wanted. They visited a couple of stores and Sarah found the perfect dress. It was light blue with white ruffles around the sleeves, the collar and the hem. When she tried it on, Mrs. Brown thought she looked so beautiful in it.

"Granny this is it. I love it," Sarah said.

"It was made just for you. You look so beautiful in it," Mrs. Brown said.

"Thank you, Granny. I love you so much," Sarah said.

"You are very welcome and you deserve the best and I love you too," Mrs. Brown replied.

Well it's only three days before Sarah's birthday and she has not heard from her parents. She's beginning to feel that she probably won't see them. Sarah was getting sad again and Mrs. Brown noticed it and told her to cheer up.

"You have three more days before your party. Always keep hope alive. God is working wonders every day," Mrs. Brown said.

Sarah hugged her Grandmother and said, "I don't know what I would have done without you. You always make me feel better when I am sad."

Mrs. Brown met with Marvin for lunch on that Friday at Johnny's Restaurant close to their office. She arrived about two minutes ahead of Marvin. When he came into the parking lot, he saw her car so he was able to park next to her. Marvin got out and went to Mrs. Brown's car and opened her door for her. He took her hand and helped her get out of the car. They hugged each other for a long time.

"Beverly told me that she explained everything to you. I am sorry that I didn't trust you enough to come and talk with you first. I love Beverly and

Sarah more than life itself. I am not going to lose my family," Marvin said.

"Sometimes we have to go through some rough spots to realize what we have and how blessed we are," Mrs. Brown said. "I know that you love Beverly and Sarah."

"I've learned a lot this past year. I have prayed and stood still. It has made me realize that it doesn't matter who is right or wrong but the better person must give in for the benefit of the family. It wasn't worth losing my family and we both are very sorry for what we put Sarah through. We will never be able to erase that from her memory," Marvin said.

"Marvin, I love you like my son. The best advice that I can give you is always take your problems and concern to God. You and Beverly have to remember to keep a line of communication open. If you don't talk to each other, you won't know the other one's concerns. Most problems between couples can be worked out if they will listen to the other person," Mrs. Brown said. "Listening is very important."

"I promise if I ever have a serious problem again, you will be the one that I call. You are a very wise woman," Marvin said.

"You learn as you live," Mrs. Brown said. "I am so happy to see you. I have been praying for you and Beverly to work out your differences. Sarah has been very hurt by this but she is a survivor."

"Thank you, Mom. I love you so much," Marvin said.

After Marvin and Mrs. Brown ate lunch, they talked a little while longer. Then Marvin had to get back to the office. He walked Mrs. Brown to her car and hugged her.

"Mom, I am so happy that I found Beverly and you and Papa," Marvin said. "You can't imagine what you all mean to me. I have my Dad but we don't have the kind of relationship that I had with Papa. I really miss him."

"I know it is something that you never get over, you just adjust to it. He is always on my mind. He was my best friend also," Mrs. Brown said.

"Well I have to get back to the office. I will see you tomorrow. We will be about twenty minutes late to give Sarah's friends time to arrive. I can hardly wait to see her," Marvin said.

"She told me that she prayed that she would see both of you on her birthday," Mrs. Brown said.

"After Saturday, she won't have to worry about anything like this happening again," Marvin said. "Kiss Sarah for me and I will talk with you later."

In the meantime, Marvin has moved back home with Beverly and they are happy and plan to stay that way. They have decided that when they have a problem, they will pray about it. Sarah is going to be surprised at the way her room has been remodeled. Beverly is going to let her pick out her clothes when they go shopping.

Marvin plans to train Sarah in bookkeeping and teach her computer skills. One day their businesses will be Sarah's. She is already a very intelligent little girl and she learns fast. He is excited about her coming home.

Marvin and Beverly have missed Sarah. Now they are going to be a family again. Sarah is going to miss her Grandmother but she will be able to see and visit her regularly.

Beverly told Marvin, "I can't wait to see Sarah's reaction to her room and her gifts."

"I know that she will love everything," Marvin said. "Our little girl is growing up."

"Yes and before we know it, she will be courting," Beverly said.

"I don't think so," Marvin said. "I will prolong that as long as I can."

"Yeah right," Beverly said. They started laughing.

"Well this is one father, the date is going to have an interview, "Marvin said.

Beverly started laughing so hard, she couldn't believe what she was hearing. Tears were rolling down her cheeks, she was laughing so hard.

"I hope you know that I am not kidding," Marvin said.

"Why don't you do it the way my Dad did with you?" Beverly said.

"No, it will be a whole new generation," Marvin said. "I can already see the changes now."

"Honey I hope you won't be the kind of father that scare the boys off," Beverly said.

"That's exactly what I want to do," Marvin said.

He and Beverly were laughing now.

"You are too much. That's why I love you," Beverly said.

Marvin went and hugged her and said," You are the best and that's why I love you so much."

Chapter 11

A Miracle for Sarah

Sarah had been doing a count-down of the days before her party. The night before her party, she prayed and asked God to please let her parents come and celebrate her 12th birthday with her. The next morning was Saturday. Sarah woke with anxiety and excitement about her day.

Mrs. Brown was already up and had fixed breakfast. Sarah went in the kitchen and Mrs. Brown walked over and hugged her.

She said, "Happy birthday my little Angel. I can't believe that you are now twelve years old."

"Thank you granny and I thank God for letting me see today. I prayed last night that my parents would visit me today," Sarah said.

Mrs. Brown felt a pain in her heart because she could not spoiled Sarah's surprise.

No matter what happens, you know God is in control. You have to stay happy so your guest will be happy," Mrs. Brown said.

"I know and I will be happy and enjoy myself today," Sarah said.

Beverly had invited all of Sarah's friends from their neighborhood. Sarah will have all kind of surprises today. This will be the best birthday that she has ever had.

Marvin and Beverly have remodeled Sarah's bedroom. It now looks more for a big girl's room rather than for a little girl room. They bought her a computer and a cell phone. Beverly got rid of all her little girl clothes. She plans to take her shopping so she can buy clothes like the twelve year old girls are wearing. Beverly always told Sarah to wear her dresses to the knees.

Sarah will be a teenager in a year. Her Mother is teaching her how to be a young respectful lady. Beverly and Marvin are getting excited about seeing Sarah and her expression when she finds out that they are going to take her home. Mrs. Brown has ordered a big birthday cake with Sarah's name and her picture on it. She has the backyard nicely decorated too.

The party is to be from 4:00 p.m.-8:00 p.m. There is a bounce house, ping pong table, all kind of board games, and a big Pinata filled with all kinds of wrapped candy. Sarah is doing her best to keep a smile on her face. She is still praying that her parents will come to her party. All the children have started arriving and bringing gifts. Mrs. Brown had a table just for the gifts.

Marvin and Beverly had **A Special Envelope for Sarah.** On the front of it, is written **A Miracle for Sarah.** In the envelope is a letter to her. Marvin and Beverly are apologizing to her for what they have put her through. They promised no matter what happens this will never happen again. And it says, "If you forgive us, we will take you home with us to live happily ever after. You are loved and will forever be loved by the both of us. We are family and will never be apart from each other again. You are our baby and we love you beyond measure." Love Daddy and Mommy!

Sarah kept looking for her parents but she

did not let on that she was unhappy. Marvin and Beverly told Mrs. Brown that they would come in the backyard when they started hitting the Pinata. They would wait until it was Sarah's turn so she would be blind folded.

"That would be perfect but don't be surprised if she starts crying," Mrs. Brown said.

"We all will probably be crying. We really have missed her," Marvin and Beverly said at the same time."

Marvin and Beverly got there at 4:00 p.m. and Mrs. Brown took them to her room. They could peep out the bedroom window and see the children in the yard. After an hour when all the children had arrived, Mrs. Brown announced that they would burst the Pinata. She had the children to line up. Jessica, Marsh and Sarah were together in line.

Mrs. Brown had the children in groups of five to see which group would burst the Pinata. There would be a special prize for that group. There were five groups. Sarah's group was last. After all the other children had tried to burst the Pinata, now it was Sarah's group turn. The two children before Marsha and Jessica could not burst it. Then Marsha and Jessica could not burst it. Now it was Sarah's turn. Her parents came outside.

Sarah hit the Pinata three times and could not burst it. Each child had three tries. Then Marvin stepped up behind Sarah and said swing one more time. He helped her swing and the Pinata burst open and candy fell on the patio. Sarah took her mask off real quick and looked right in Marvin's face. She jumped in his arms and started crying.

"It's alright baby. I love you," Marvin said.

"Happy Birthday, Baby," Beverly said.

She was right beside Marvin. Sarah opened her eyes and reached for Beverly. This was the happiest day of Sarah's life. Both of her parents came to her Birthday Party.

Sarah stopped crying and said, "Thank you, Jesus."

"We have a special envelope for you on the table. After you read it, give us your answer," Beverly said.

Sarah went to the table and got the envelope with her name on it. She opened it and read it. Then she ran to her parents, hugging both of them.

"My answer is yes! Yes!" Sarah said. "I am going home with my parents. I am going home!"

Everyone was clapping for her and tears were

in the eyes of most of her guest including the adults. Sarah went and hugged her Grandmother.

"You said, "Never give up on hope. Thank you, Jesus. Thank you, God," Sarah shouted. "And thank you Granny. I love all of you so much."

This was the best birthday party that Sarah ever had. Although her biggest surprise was after she got home. When the party was over, she had bid farewell to all of her guests. Now it was time to say good bye to her Nanny. Sarah was going to miss her friends. She didn't know that her parents had already made plans for her to continue going to her school until the semester ended. They lived about ten minutes from Mrs. Brown so she would be able to visit her friends and they could visit her also.

One of her parents would take her to school in the morning and the other one would pick her up after school. If they could not do it, Mrs. Brown would fill in. The best blessing for Sara was that she lived ten minutes away from her Granny. She would be able spend the night sometime on the weekends with her friends or they could spend the night with her.

The best part of her transition, she would not

have to give up her bowling or her new friends. When Sarah's friends found out that they would still be able to bowl with her, they were overjoyed. When they got home that night, Sarah just cried when she walked into the house.

"What's the matter baby?" Marvin asked.

"I am just so happy to be back with you and Mom," Sarah said. "I was beginning to think you all didn't want me anymore."

Tears came in Beverly and Marvin's eyes. They both hugged Sarah and they all cried.

"Honey, we are so sorry for putting you through that. We promised, no matter what, it will never happen again," Beverly said.

"Baby, we love you and we love each other. We have made an agreement that if we ever have a problem like that again, we will pray together about it," Marvin said.

"And we will talk to your Granny about it because she is a very wise woman," Beverly said. "And there will be some things that we will be able to discuss with you and get your opinion."

"We are family and we will do things as a family. You are growing and is pretty wise, so we will ask for your input in things sometime," Marvin said.

"We don't ever want you to think that we don't love or want you. You are a blessing from God and we cherish you," Beverly said.

"Mom, Dad, I love you all so much," Sarah said.

"Now that we have that out of the way, we have one more big surprise for you," Marvin said.

"Where is it?" Sarah asked.

"Follow us," Beverly said. "We hope you really like it and will enjoy it to the fullest."

When Marvin opened Sarah's bedroom door, she could not believe what she was seeing. She started going around in the room touching everything in awe. She was so happy to see the new decoration and her gifts.

After she checked everything out, she turned to her parents with tears rolling down her cheeks.

"You all have made me so happy. The best gift is my miracle, putting my family back together. I love you all so much," Sarah said. "I don't think that I am going to be able to sleep tonight."

"Don't worry about it. You can stay up tonight as long as you like. We will be up with you. We are just excited as you for you to be home," Beverly said.

"We have missed you so much. Now that you

are growing up, sometimes on a Saturday, we will take you to the office so you can start learning how it operates," Marvin said.

"You know, one day, the business will be yours," Marvin said.

"Really!" Sarah replied.

"Yes. You are our only child and if you outlive us, it will be yours. In the meantime, when you are a couple of years older, you will be able to work part time in the office," Marvin said.

"You will be able to earn your own money so you can learn how to manage it. When you are ready to leave home, you will already know how to handle your money," Beverly said.

"That sounds exciting. I will be able to work and earn money. I like that idea," Sarah said.

Marvin and Beverly looked at each other and laughed.

"Why are you all laughing?" Sarah asked.

"After you start working, you may have a little change of idea. Some people like working and some don't. Those that don't will hardly ever have anything," Marvin said.

"I won't mind working because I am going to successful in whatever I do," Sarah said. "And I will do my best in everything that I do."

"That's my girl," Marvin said. "I love the fact that you are always thinking positive."

"That's the way you get ahead, Dad," Sarah said.

"Ok now we can go and sit down and chat," Beverly said. "Welcome back home baby."

"We have a lot of catching up to do," Marvin said. "We have missed you so much."

"I thank God that we are home and are a family again. This has been my prayer and God answered it. Thank you, Jesus!" Sarah said.

Bio

oris M. Jones was born in Dallas, Texas. Her family moved to California in 1965. She is the Mother of five adult children, grandmother of eleven and great-grandmother of thirteen. She lived in Fresno-Clovis, CA area for fifteen years and moved back to Southern Cal in 1999.

She's a published Author of eight books. She has about seventy poems published in different Anthologies in the Public Libraries. This is her ninth book. She loves going to church, family gatherings and her passion is writing.

Doris is always willing to help someone in need if she can.

P.S. Doris´ poems are under former name Jones-Landrine in the Poetry Anthologies.

Printed in the United States
by Baker & Taylor Publisher Services

Printed in the United States
by Baker & Taylor Publisher Services